tuffy

STORY
BOOKS

Alice in Wonderland
Sleeping Beauty
Puss in Boots
The Ugly Duckling
The Pied Piper of Hamelin
Ali Baba and the Forty Thieves
Pinocchio
Peter Pan
Cinderella
The Princess and the Pea
Sinbad the Sailor
Little Red Riding Hood

TUFFY BOOKS, INC., HARRISON, N.Y.
Copyright©1987 by Tuffy Books, Inc. All rights reserved.
Tuffy©, Tuffy Story Books© are trademarks of Tuffy Books, Inc.
©R.B.A. Proyectos Editoriales, S.A. ©copyright 1983, 1987.
Printed in Singapore

Alice in Wonderland

Lewis Carroll

Once upon a time, on a hot summer day, a little girl named Alice sat beneath a big tree enjoying the shade.

A White Rabbit suddenly ran by. He stopped just long enough to glance at his watch before he disappeared into the woods.

"That's not possible!" Alice exclaimed. Without thinking twice, she ran after the incredible White Rabbit who had scurried into a big hole in the ground.

Alice tumbled into the hole. She fell through a long, dark tunnel. She landed at the bottom on a pile of dry leaves.

Alice rubbed her eyes in wonder. She found herself in an extraordinary room with many doors. In the center of the room was a three-legged glass table. On the table was a small gold key and a bottle. A label on the bottle said, "Drink me."

Alice used the gold key to open one of the tiny doors. On the other side was a beautiful garden.

Alice was too big to go through the door. She didn't know quite what to do, so she drank from the bottle that said, "Drink me."

To her surprise, Alice began to shrink. Soon she was small enough to go through the door.

But she forgot the key on the table. Now she was too small to reach it. Alice began to cry.

In an instant she grew so tall her head bumped the ceiling! She grabbed the key and became small again.

On the other side of the door was a pond made of Alice's own tears. A little Mouse helped her to swim across the pond.

On the opposite shore Alice met a Dodo, a Duck, a Parrot and some other animals who gave her a thimble as a sign of welcome.

As she wandered through the marvelous land, Alice wondered how she could return to her normal size.

"How I can grow big again?" she asked a Blue Caterpillar on a mushroom smoking a pipe.

"Eat a piece of the right side of the mushroom to stay small," the Blue Caterpillar said. "Eat some from the left side and you'll grow."

Alice took a tiny piece from each side of the mushroom so she could grow or shrink according to her wishes. She thanked the Blue Caterpillar and went on her way.

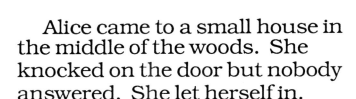

Alice came to a small house in the middle of the woods. She knocked on the door but nobody answered. She let herself in.

Alice stepped into the kitchen. In the center of the room was a Duchess with a crying baby in her arms. The Duchess was quite unpleasant.

The Cook poured soup on the floor where a Chesire Cat sat with a big grin on its face.

The Duchess didn't know how to smile. She threw the Baby at Alice. The Baby landed on the floor and turned into a Little Pig that trotted out the door.

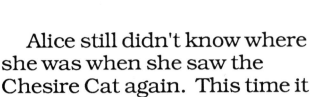

Alice still didn't know where she was when she saw the Chesire Cat again. This time it sat in the branch of a tree.

"Go in that direction to meet the Mad Hatter and the March Hare," said the Chesire Cat. Then it vanished like a puff of smoke.

Alice followed the Chesire Cat's directions. She arrived in a clearing in the woods where the Mad Hatter, the March Hare and a Doormouse sat at a table having a tea party.

Alice sat in an empty chair. She served herself some bread and butter.

The Doormouse said very little. All it wanted to do was sleep. But the Mad Hatter and the March Hare wouldn't stop talking. They talked so fast that Alice couldn't understand a word they said.

Soon Alice left the strange tea party and returned to the path.

A short time later, Alice arrived at a beautiful garden filled with pure white roses. In a corner three odd looking fellows were painting the white roses red.

The little girl stared at the men in surprise. They were playing cards that had come to life!

"What are you doing?" asked Alice.

"The Queen of Hearts wants red rose bushes in her garden," they replied. "But we made a mistake. We planted white roses. If we paint them red, she won't know the difference. Then she won't punish us."

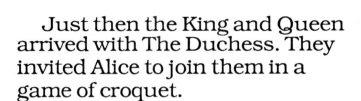

Just then the King and Queen
arrived with The Duchess. They
invited Alice to join them in a
game of croquet.

The balls were tiny hedgehogs.
The mallets were pink flamingos.
Alice couldn't play that way. That
made the Queen very angry.

The Queen ordered her guards to arrest Alice. They took the poor girl to court to be punished for not knowing anything.

The White Rabbit returned blowing a big trumpet. He called to Alice.

Alice was frightened. She ate a piece of the mushroom that made her grow big again.

When the Queen saw that, she ordered her guards to attack.

The guards surrounded Alice, but they were small and she was very big.

"You're only playing cards," Alice said. "I'm not afraid of you."

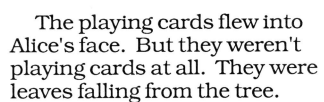

The playing cards flew into
Alice's face. But they weren't
playing cards at all. They were
leaves falling from the tree.
Alice had fallen asleep. The
wonderland was just a dream!